Butterfly Dreams

written by MELISSA ANN WINTER

tate publishing
CHILDREN'S DIVISION

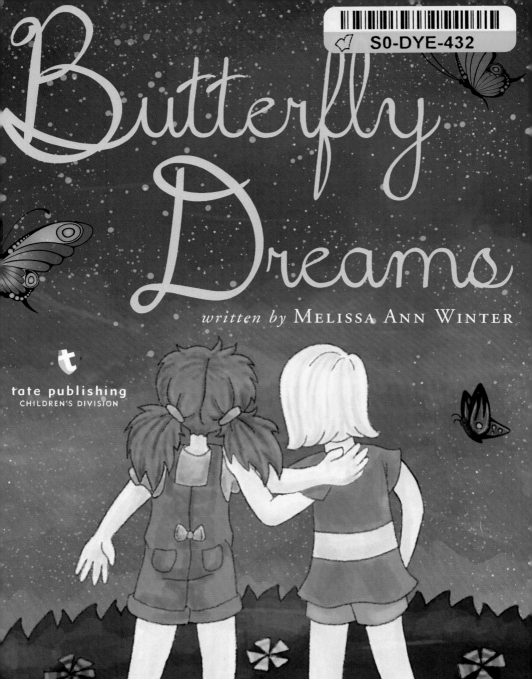

Published by Tate Publishing & Enterprises, LLC
127 E. Trade Center Terrace | Mustang, Oklahoma 73064 USA
1.888.361.9473 | www.tatepublishing.com

Tate Publishing is committed to excellence in the publishing industry. The company reflects the philosophy established by the founders, based on Psalm 68:11,
"The Lord gave the word and great was the company of those who published it."

Book design copyright © 2012 by Tate Publishing, LLC. All rights reserved.
Cover and interior design by Chris Webb
Illustrations by Julie Love Yarbor

Published in the United States of America
ISBN: 978-1-61862-838-1
1. Juvenile Fiction / Animals / Butterflies, Moths & Caterpillars
2. Juvenile Fiction / Social Issues / Death & Dying
12.03.26

For Kathi

Illustrations inspired by Peggy L. Fox

Acknowledgments

To KRW and family. You are right; I have never felt as much love as I do when I am with my little ones.

To my best friend, Peggy. With your amazing talents, your loving heart, and positive energy, I am so blessed.

To Mike, my love and my friend, for being my added kick in the pants to get moving force in my life. What would I ever do without you?

To Kathi. Your courage, strength, and determination with your past two fights against cancer and now the mesothelioma has made me realize the importance of time and become a huge part of the urgency to get this published. Thank you for being my sister, and my friend all these years. I will do my best to always honor you by living my life with your courage and grace.

Once upon a time, there were two little girls, each from a different place.

Allie and Maddy were best friends. Oh, how they talked and shared their hopes and dreams and their darkest fears.

Life was good for Allie and Maddy, who, until they had met, had each been without a best friend. Now they had one another!

One day, in their daydreaming, Allie said, "I love butterflies. They get to go all over the world. Someday, I would like to go all over the world like a butterfly."

Maddy looked up in the sky as she lay in the soft grass. "Yes! That would be so fun, to see everything and everyone from up above, like an angel or a butterfly."

Allie asked Maddy, "Maddy, do you suppose butterflies are angels sent to remind us that loved ones are always near, just like God's love?"

Allie sighed. "I think they are. If I was to someday become an angel, I would want to be a butterfly to come back to earth to see you and make sure you were not sad because you are my best friend in the whole world. I would never want anything to make you sad."

As the two girls lay in the summer grass with the warm wind blowing, a monarch butterfly drifted by and landed on a dandelion, and she smiled at the two girls.

One day, Allie became very ill and went up to heaven. Maddy felt so alone and scared, thinking she would never find another best friend to share her hopes and dreams with. Maddy was very sad.

School and play time that she used to enjoy felt so empty now.

Spring came, and Maddy was sitting on her steps when a soft wind began to blow. Maddy stood up and walked over to the tree under which she and Allie used to sit.

As she sat there, she lay down and said, "Oh, Allie, I miss you so much."

As she lay there, she closed her eyes and the tears fell from her cheeks to the ground. There, along side of her, bloomed a rose, a rose grown out of the tears of love for a best friend deeply missed.

When Maddy opened her eyes, she touched the rose in wonder. But even more amazing is that as she touched the rose, a monarch butterfly fluttered by and landed on Maddy's hand.

Maddy looked quietly at the butterfly, and the butterfly began to speak. "When you are lonely, I am there beside you. When you get scared at night, I will hold you tight. When you laugh, I will always laugh with you. I am free to fly anywhere in the world, and by your side is where I will always be, for heaven is timeless and so is God's love for you."

"Mine too," whispered Maddy as she held the butterfly gently.

"Live your life, Maddy, for someday, you will find love and joy like you have never known. And remember, you didn't lose me. Whenever you see a butterfly, think of me and I will be there. I am only a thought away."

At that point, the butterfly flew up and landed on the rose. The rose turned the most beautiful red with dewdrops on its petals. "Turn your tears of sorrow to tears of hope." From there, the butterfly flew up and up 'til it flew out of Maddy's sight.

"Maddy! Lunch is ready."

"Mom, I was talking with Allie! She was a butterfly, and she came and there was this rose."

Maddy's mom looked softly down at her daughter and took her hand. As they walked, her mom said, "Yes, those we love who have gone to heaven are never far away."

Outside, by the tree where Maddy and Allie used to dream their dreams stood the rose and, on its petals, a monarch butterfly. And she smiled.

Afterword

"Your best friend is the one friend that you take with you in your heart and in your life's travels no matter the distance; a best friend is someone you never leave behind."

—Melissa A. Winter

e|LIVE

listen|imagine|view|experience

AUDIO BOOK DOWNLOAD INCLUDED WITH THIS BOOK!

In your hands you hold a complete digital entertainment package. In addition to the paper version, you receive a free download of the audio version of this book. Simply use the code listed below when visiting our website. Once downloaded to your computer, you can listen to the book through your computer's speakers, burn it to an audio CD or save the file to your portable music device (such as Apple's popular iPod) and listen on the go!

How to get your free audio book digital download:

1. Visit www.tatepublishing.com and click on the e|LIVE logo on the home page.
2. Enter the following coupon code:
   e622-f1ff-602a-bb20-1524-ef66-9645-5a90
3. Download the audio book from your e|LIVE digital locker and begin enjoying your new digital entertainment package today!